DUCKLING DIARY

Books in the *Animal Ark Pets* series

Ben M. Baglio

DUCKLING DIARY

Illustrated by
John Speirs

Cover illustration by
Chris Chapman

A
LITTLE APPLE
PAPERBACK

SCHOLASTIC INC.

New York Toronto London Auckland Sydney
Mexico City New Delhi Hong Kong

Special thanks to Sue Welford

ISBN 0-439-05167-3

12 11 10 9 8 7 6 5 4 3 2 1   0 1 2 3 4 5/0

Printed in the U.S.A.   40

First Scholastic Trade paperback printing, April 2000

Contents

1

An Exciting Discovery

"There she is!" Mandy Hope whispered excitedly. "She's coming back."

Mandy and her best friend, James Hunter, were lying on their stomachs in the long grass overlooking Millers Pond.

James's young Labrador dog, Blackie, was with them.

They were all watching a mallard's nest. The mother duck had just returned after leaving it for a few minutes to feed.

Mandy and James had been watching the duck for weeks now. First they saw her building her nest. She gathered sticks and reeds and wove them into a beautiful nest on a small island just off the bank. Then she laid her eggs, keeping them warm, sitting patiently, and quietly waiting for them to hatch.

Today was the first time Mandy and James were able to see how many eggs lay snugly in the nest. There were five, and Mandy was delighted.

"Five eggs!" she whispered. "Five babies! Oh, James, I just can't wait."

Mandy was studying the duck for a project her class was doing at school. When Mrs. Todd first told the students that they were each to study an animal or bird for a class project, Mandy didn't know what to do. She didn't have a pet of her own to study.

Some of Mandy's classmates who had pets came up with ideas right away. Mandy heard her friends already giving their projects names, such as *Gerbil Journal*, *Rabbit Record*, and *Hamster History*.

Then Mandy and James discovered the mallard's nest, and her problem was solved. She was going to write a *Duckling Diary*!

After every visit she wrote about the duck in her project book. When the ducklings hatched she intended to keep a record of them, too.

Now Mandy and James watched the duck settle down. She preened herself for a little while, then sat contentedly in her nest. The bright spring sunshine warmed her gleaming pale brown feathers.

James sighed. "I wonder when they're going to hatch. It seems as if she's been sitting there forever."

"I know," Mandy said. "I hope it's soon."

"Come on," James whispered. "We'd better go before she spots us."

Mandy didn't want to leave. Lying there in the grass, with the sun shining and the bees buzzing from wildflower to wildflower, Mandy felt as if she were in heaven.

James was right. It was great to watch wildlife, but you had to be careful not to interfere.

So they crept quietly away.

James held tightly to Blackie's leash. The last thing he wanted was for Blackie to have one of his bursts of energy and go charging around.

The sky was a deep, vivid blue as Mandy and James ran along the field's edge and out into the lane to make their way home.

Mandy and James lived in the village of Welford, where Mandy's parents were the local vets. Their clinic was attached to the stone cottage where the family lived. The clinic was called Animal Ark.

As they were going by the village green, Mandy suddenly realized there wasn't much point in going home yet. Her mom would be busy at the clinic this time of day, and her dad would be out on his calls. "Wait," she said.

"What?" James stopped beside her. He pushed his glasses back up on his nose and jerked Blackie away from a cat that had innocently crossed his path.

"Why don't we go to Lilac Cottage and tell Grandma and Grandpa?" Mandy suggested.

"Tell them what?" James asked.

"About the five eggs, silly. Don't you think it's a good idea?"

James nodded. "You bet."

Visiting Mandy's grandparents was always a good idea. Mandy's grandma made the best cookies and lemonade in the whole world.

"Come on," he added. "Race you."

Mandy laughed as James ran off. His legs were going a mile a minute. Blackie pulled him as fast as could be.

"It's not fair," she shouted when he surged on ahead.

James managed to stop the puppy and stood waiting for her. "Sorry," he grinned. "But I

could probably still beat you even without Blackie's help."

Mandy grinned back. It was great having a friend like James. Not only did he love animals as much as she did, he let her share Blackie, too. She really wanted to have pets of her own but knew it was impossible. The Hope family was so busy looking after other people's animals, there just wasn't time to look after any of their own.

She grabbed Blackie's leash from James's hand and ran on ahead, calling over her shoulder. "Now, let's see who wins!"

They arrived at the cottage gate together.

"What on earth's going on!" Grandma exclaimed when they both burst through the back door, giggling and laughing. Blackie flopped down on the floor, panting.

Mandy explained about their race. Then she asked, "Guess what, Grandma?"

"Now, calm down, Mandy." Grandma looked as if she was just about to go out, but she always had time to listen to her grand-daughter. "What's all the excitement about?"

"Eggs!" Mandy and James said together.

"Eggs?" Grandma looked puzzled.

"In the nest," Mandy said. "You know, the one on Millers Pond."

"Oh, the *duck's* nest," Grandma said. "Five! My goodness, the mother's going to be busy, isn't she?"

"Busy?" Grandpa came in from the garden. "I'm always busy."

Mandy laughed and explained that they weren't talking about him.

Grandpa was carrying a basket of early potatoes. He had mud all over his shoes. Grandma frowned when he came into the kitchen without taking them off. He bent down and quickly untied the laces. He gave his wife a grin. "Sorry, Dorothy." He winked at James. "How are you, James?"

"Good, thanks," James said.

Grandpa bent down to pat Blackie, while

Mandy explained about the nest and the pond and the eggs.

"Millers Pond . . ." Grandpa smiled. "I used to go there when I was a boy. My pals and I made a raft once. It sank the first time out. My, did we get into trouble for getting our clothes all wet. I remember . . ."

Mandy tapped her fingers impatiently. She loved hearing Grandpa's stories. But not now. Now she wanted to know about duck eggs.

"Grandpa," she said quickly, "do you know how long duck eggs take to hatch?"

"Um . . . no, I don't, honey. Sorry." He put the basket on the drain board and scrubbed his hands under the faucet. "Do you know, Dorothy?" he asked Grandma.

She shook her head. "No, sorry. I have no idea." She glanced at her watch and then planted a quick kiss on top of Mandy's head. "I must go. My friend Kathy is expecting me. We're organizing a Women's Club visit to that new farm park just outside the village."

"I saw an ad for it in the local paper," James said. "It's called Woodbridge Farm Park."

"That's right," Grandma said. "It used to be an ordinary farm, but the new owners have turned it into a place where the public can go to see how a farm works. Our club is going to have a guided tour, and we've got a few more details to settle."

"Are there lots of animals?" Mandy asked.

"I believe so. And poultry. Kathy has lots of chickens, so she'll be especially interested."

"I'll take you and James one day, if you like," Grandpa said.

Mandy's eyes shone. "That would be great, wouldn't it, James?"

"Yes." James was trying not to look sad. He was disappointed when he saw that Mandy's Grandma was going out. His vision of home-made cookies and lemonade was disappearing fast.

Grandma must have noticed. "Help yourself to something to eat," she told them with a twinkle in her eye.

Mandy gave her a swift hug. "Thanks, Grandma."

When she left, Mandy turned to her grandpa.

"Won't it be great, Grandpa? Five ducklings!"

"Wonderful," Grandpa said. He was looking in the pantry for the cookie tin. He found it, opened the lid, and put it on the kitchen table in front of them. Blackie sat up when his nose caught the scent.

"Mind you," Grandpa added, "you'd better keep Blackie under control. Labradors are inclined to chase ducks, you know."

James *did* know. Labradors were inclined to chase anything that moved. "We will," he assured him.

"Good." Grandpa opened the refrigerator door and took out a tall pitcher of pale lemonade. "Because the mother duck will desert the nest if she gets scared."

Mandy looked at James in horror. "We won't let that happen, honestly, Grandpa!"

When they finished their snack, washed their glasses and plates, admired Grandpa's potatoes, and inspected his tomato plants, Mandy and James headed home.

They split up at the village green, because James lived on the other side of the village.

"Let's go back first thing tomorrow," Mandy suggested.

"Sure," James replied. "And I'll threaten Blackie with no dinner if he doesn't behave himself."

Mandy grinned. "Okay, see you tomorrow!"

2

Good Boy, Blackie!

The mobile library van was parked by the village green. Peggy, the librarian, was helping one of Welford's elderly residents down the steps.

"Hi, Mandy," she called when she saw Mandy hurrying past. "Don't you want any books today?"

Mandy halted. Maybe Peggy had a book about ducks. She walked across the green and up the van steps. Inside were racks of books and a little desk where Peggy checked people's library cards and stamped the books with the date the books had to be returned.

"Have you got any books about ducks, please?" Mandy asked.

Peggy went to look on the shelves and came back with *All You Need to Know About Ducks.* She handed it to Mandy.

It was just what Mandy wanted. "Oh, that's perfect. Thanks, Peggy." Then her face fell. "Oh . . . I don't have my library card with me."

Peggy smiled. "Don't worry. I'll look your number up on the computer when I get back to Walton Library." She took a rubber stamp and stamped the inside of the book. "Why do you want a book about ducks?"

Mandy explained.

"*Five* eggs, how wonderful!" Peggy said. "Well, good luck with the ducklings."

"Thanks," Mandy said. She tucked the book under her arm and set off for home.

Back at Animal Ark, Mandy's mom had just finished her morning clinic hours. Dr. Emily Hope was in the kitchen, sitting with her feet up on a chair and drinking a cup of coffee, when Mandy burst in with her news.

"What a day!" she said to Mandy with a sigh. "Five cats, three dogs, a budgie, a gerbil, and a lizard."

"A lizard!" Mandy exclaimed. "That's unusual."

"Yes. Tommy Day from that house next to the general store found a lizard without a tail on his garden wall. He was really worried, but I assured him it would grow a new one."

Mandy told her mom about the eggs and showed her the book she had borrowed from the library van.

"Great," Dr. Emily said. "But you'll have to be very careful not to disturb the mother."

"Oh, we will," Mandy said. "We *are* being very careful already."

"That's good." Dr. Emily got up and put her cup into the dishwasher. "Well, sweetheart, duty calls. I'll see you later." She gave Mandy a kiss on top of her head. "Dad's in the clinic if you need him." She picked up her bag and went out.

Mandy went upstairs to her room to lie on her bed and study the book about ducks. When she came to the page that told about eggs hatching, she sat up. She ran to her desk to check her project book.

It was almost six weeks ago that she and James first spotted the duck building her nest. Two weeks to build it . . . four weeks to sit on the eggs. She looked at the dates, carefully written down since that first day. Her heart pounded with excitement as she worked the dates out.

She ran downstairs to the phone and quickly dialed James's number.

"James," she said before he'd even had a chance to say hello. "The eggs. They're due to hatch tomorrow!"

"Tomorrow!" James said. "That's great!"

"Come over as early as you can," Mandy said.

"I will," James said. "Definitely."

The following morning, Mandy was up bright and early. The warm mist promised another fine spring day. She waited eagerly at the gate for James and soon spotted him rushing down the street. Blackie was bounding ahead of James.

"Won't it be great if the eggs really do hatch today?" James's voice was full of excitement.

"Yes!" Mandy said. "My book said incubation varies from twenty-eight to thirty days. Today's the twenty-eighth day, I'm sure. So let's keep our fingers crossed."

When they approached the pond, they suddenly heard a terrible, frantic quacking and splashing. Then a beating of wings. They saw a duck fly up and away toward the cornfield, shrieking in terror.

Mandy looked at James in horror. "That's our duck!" she cried. "Quick!"

They ran as fast as they could through the long grass toward the pond.

At the water's edge, a terrible scene met their eyes. Mandy's hand flew to her mouth, and she stood there in stunned silence.

"Oh, no!" James exclaimed in a horrified voice.

The little bankside island was empty. It *was* the mother duck they had seen. Her nest had been destroyed, and she had flown away. There was no sign of the eggs. All that was left were reeds and twigs floating around the island in sad little bundles.

"Poor duck!" Mandy wailed. "What will she do now?" Tears rolled down her cheeks.

Blackie came and licked her hand. He always seemed to know when people were upset.

James was almost crying, too. "Who could have done it?" he asked, shaking his head.

Suddenly, Blackie bounded off toward the little island. There didn't seem to be much point in going after him. The duck had been frightened away already. Blackie sniffed around

in the long grass for a minute and then came trotting back.

Mandy was still sobbing.

"I bet it was a fox," James said.

"Yes," Mandy agreed tearfully. "I know foxes have to eat, but why did a fox have to attack *our* duck?"

Blackie placed something on the grass in front of Mandy. Then he nudged her knee. It was an egg. A duck egg. A perfect, unbroken duck egg.

Forgetting her tears, Mandy picked it up and cradled it gently in her hands. It was still warm! "Oh, James," she whispered.

James stared at the egg, and gave Blackie a big hug. "Good boy, Blackie!"

"James," Mandy said urgently. "Do you remember when Libby Masters's pet hen, Rhonda, was hatching her chicks? Rhonda could only leave the eggs for a few minutes, otherwise they would get cold, and the chicks inside would die."

James nodded. "Yes," he said. "We've got to keep this egg warm and get it somewhere it can stay warm as fast as we can, so the baby duck inside doesn't die."

"Grandma and Grandpa are closest," Mandy said.

"Right," James replied. "Come on!"

With Mandy holding the egg in both hands close to her body for warmth, they hurried toward Lilac Cottage.

Grandpa was surprised to see the three of them so early in the day, although he had been up for a while. He was in his greenhouse tying up a web of string to support his budding tomato plants. Grandma had just gone out shopping.

"What on earth's wrong?" Grandpa asked when he saw their anxious faces.

"Oh, Grandpa!" Mandy quickly told him what had happened. "Where can we put the egg to keep it warm?"

"The linen closet should do for the time be-ing," Grandpa replied.

They all hurried indoors. Mandy walked carefully up the stairs and placed the egg on a bundle of Grandma's snowy white towels on the shelf nearest the hot water tank.

"That should do it," she murmured. She touched the shell gently with her fingertip. "Now, you keep nice and warm, baby duck. We're going to look after you, so you needn't worry." She closed the linen closet door softly and ran back downstairs.

Grandpa and James were sitting at the kitchen table.

"Well," Grandpa said. "Now what are you going to do?"

3

Keeping Warm

Mandy shook her head. She knew that eggs had to be kept at the right warm temperature to hatch, but how, when there was no mother duck to do the job?

"Why don't we call Libby Masters's dad?" James suggested. "He has chickens, but he might know about ducks, too."

"That's a great idea, James!" Mandy replied. "Let's call him now. May we, Grandpa?"

"Of course," her grandpa replied. "The number should be in the phone book."

Mandy hurried into the hall, then found and dialed the number for Blackheath Farm. It rang and rang. No one was in. She sighed and went back into the kitchen. "No answer," she told them unhappily.

Then Mandy's face suddenly lit up. "*I* know!" she said. "Grandma's friend Kathy! Grandma told us she has chickens, too, so *she* might be able to tell us what to do next."

"Good thinking," Grandpa said. "I'll call her and ask."

Grandpa seemed to be on the phone for ages. "Yes . . . no . . . oh, dear, I am sorry. . . . Yes, I'm sure you will. Was he? Oh, what a shame. . . . But he lived a normal life? Oh, yes, that's good . . ."

James looked at Mandy. "What are they talking about?"

Mandy shrugged. "I don't know, but it doesn't sound like ducks to me."

After a few more minutes, Grandpa called out. "Kathy wants to know when you think the egg will hatch."

"Today," Mandy said urgently. "We think it might be today."

Eventually, Grandpa came back into the kitchen. "That woman," he said. "She *does* know how to talk. She's been telling me all about her poor cat."

"What's wrong with it?" James asked.

"It died, poor thing. She's very upset."

"Oh, that's terrible," Mandy murmured. She felt sad that Kathy's cat had died, but she was desperate to know what Kathy had said about the egg. She wriggled impatiently in her chair. "Grandpa, what did she say about the . . ."

"The egg? Oh, yes, the egg." He opened one of the kitchen cabinets and took out a large glass mixing bowl. "This'll do."

"Won't Grandma mind?" Mandy asked.

"Not if it's for a good cause," Grandpa grinned. "You know Grandma is always in favor of good causes. Come on. Follow me, and I'll show you what we're going to do."

First, Grandpa went down to his compost heap and filled the bottom of the bowl with grass cuttings. They were still damp from the dew and warm from the early morning sun. Then he took it into the greenhouse.

"Kathy said the egg needs to be kept warm and slightly damp." He made a small hollow in the grass cuttings and put the bowl on the floor. Then he took his greenhouse heater, placed it near the bowl, and plugged it in.

"Kathy said to keep the egg at this constant temperature." He set the dial on the heater. "Okay, Mandy, get the egg."

Mandy ran indoors and up the stairs. She took the egg out gently and walked carefully back downstairs and out into the greenhouse.

Grandpa took the egg carefully from her and placed it in the warm nest. Then he covered the bowl with a dark cloth and turned to

Mandy and James. "Now," he said, "all we have to do is wait."

"What for?" came a voice from the doorway.

Mandy turned to see Grandma standing there. She ran toward her. "Oh, Grandma, you'll never guess what."

"Oh, dear," Grandma said when Mandy told her what had happened. "Poor duck." Grandma gazed at Grandpa. "But Kathy said it would be quite easy to hatch this egg."

"Should be," Grandpa confirmed.

"In my best mixing bowl?" Grandma asked.

Grandpa looked a bit sheepish.

"Oh, Grandma, you don't mind, do you?" Mandy cried.

Grandma smiled. "No, of course not."

Mandy clapped her hands. "Oh, Grandma. Won't it be wonderful?"

"It certainly will." She patted Mandy's arm. "You and James go and start unloading the groceries from the car. There's a good girl."

"Okay." Mandy's eyes were still shining. "Come on, James."

By the time Mandy and James had brought in the groceries, Grandma and Grandpa were back in the kitchen.

"Mandy and James kept it warm, but it was pretty shaken up," Grandpa was saying. "All we can do is wait and keep our fingers crossed."

"Oh, dear," Mandy heard Grandma say. "They'll be so upset if nothing happens."

Mandy's heart sank. By the look on Grandpa's face, she could tell he thought the egg might not hatch.

She had to go and look at the egg just to make sure it was all right.

But Grandma caught her arm as she went past. "A watched pot never boils," she said. "If you keep going to look at the egg, it will seem like ages before it hatches. Best leave it alone, Mandy. Let nature take its course."

Mandy sighed and sat down reluctantly. Grandma put the kettle on for a cup of tea and began to unpack the bags and put the groceries away. James was helping. Grandpa began telling her about Kathy's cat.

"Oh, dear," Grandma said. "The old boy did look as if he was on his last legs when I visited Kathy yesterday. She'll miss him terribly. He was deaf, you know."

"Poor thing," James said.

Grandma smiled. "Oh, Snowball led a great life. And the wonderful part was that he couldn't hear Kathy's chicks cheeping, so he didn't try to chase them. He really was the perfect cat for her."

Mandy leaned her chin on her hands and stared out of the window. She could just see the greenhouse from where she was sitting. "You *will* let me know as soon as anything happens, won't you?" she asked her grandparents anxiously.

"Yes, of course," Grandpa said.

"Even if it's in the middle of the night?" Mandy asked.

Grandma laughed. "We don't mind keeping your egg for you two. But we're not staying up all night. Not even for a duckling."

Mandy managed a grin. "I know. But could you look first thing in the morning?"

Grandma poured her tea. "Knowing you, Mandy, you'll be here before your grandpa and I are even out of bed."

"And me," James said, eyeing the cookie tin.

"Yes, James," Grandma said. "And you."

Before they left, Mandy couldn't resist having one more look at the egg. If there was a crack in the shell it would mean the duckling was starting to peck its way out.

But the egg lay there in the bowl, perfectly still, not a crack to be seen. Mandy touched the delicate shell with the tip of her finger. The book from the library van had a picture of an unborn duckling. It was curled up tight, and it filled the whole inside of the egg. Mandy could just imagine this one curled up, eyes closed, resting before it faced the big, wide world.

"Please be all right," she whispered as she touched the egg again. "Please be all right."

As she spoke the egg moved. Just a tiny bit, wobbling from side to side. Mandy blinked. Had she imagined it? She touched it again. Maybe her finger had disturbed it? But it didn't wobble again. It just lay there, warm and still.

Mandy sighed. James was waiting with Blackie at the gate. She put the dark cloth back over the bowl, went out, and closed the door softly behind her. Grandma was right again. A watched pot never boils.

4

Crossing Bridges

Dr. Adam Hope was out on a call when Mandy
arrived back at Animal Ark. Dr. Emily was in
the waiting room pinning a notice to the bul-
letin board.

"Oh, I'm sorry, Mandy," she said when she
heard about the nest. "That kind of thing often
happens in nature."

"I know," Mandy said. "But at least we might be able to save one of the baby ducks."

Her mom gave her a quick hug. "Yes, although I'm not sure what you'll do with a duckling if the egg does hatch."

Mandy didn't really want to think about that yet. *We'll cross that bridge when we come to it* was another of Grandma's favorite sayings. And that's what Mandy had decided to do.

She ran upstairs to update her project book before lunch. She wiped a tear from her eye as she wrote about the nest being destroyed. She hoped her friends wouldn't have such sad things to write about in *their* project books.

When Mandy finished writing, she looked at her library book again. At the end was a chapter about newly hatched ducklings.

"'When it hatches, a duckling will imprint on the first thing it sees,'" Mandy read. She wasn't sure what *imprint* meant, but she made up her mind to ask her mom at lunch. On the same page was a picture of a long line of fluffy yellow ducklings waddling confidently along behind their mother.

Mandy closed the book and sighed. What was her poor duckling going to do without a mother to follow?

Dr. Emily was making lunch when Mandy ran downstairs and into the kitchen. "*Imprint?*" she repeated when Mandy asked her. "It means that the first thing a duckling sees will stay in its mind, and the duckling will follow that thing everywhere. This is usually its mother, of course. It's nature's way of keeping some young creatures safe."

"Oh . . ." Mandy had started setting the table. Now she stopped, fiddling with a fork and staring into space.

Dr. Emily could see something was wrong. 'What's worrying you?" she asked gently.

Mandy sighed. "Our duckling won't have a mother to imprint upon." She looked at her mom with tears in her eyes. "Poor little thing."

Dr. Emily smiled reassuringly. "Oh, Mandy,

you know what Grandma says about crossing bridges."

"Yes," Mandy sniffed.

"Well, let's do that, shall we? Your baby duck will be safe, that's really all that matters."

Mandy smiled. "Yes, I suppose so."

The following morning Mandy was up two hours before it was time to leave for school. She'd made her lunch and had just finished eating her cereal when Dr. Adam came into the kitchen.

"You're up early, Mandy," Dr. Adam said.

She explained about going to check if the egg had hatched. Then her mom came in.

"You're up early, Mandy," she said, and Mandy had to explain all over again.

"They'll probably still be in bed," Mandy heard her mom say to her dad as she grabbed her schoolbag and hurried out.

It was another beautiful morning. The sun had risen above an early mist, and the dew on the village green sparkled like diamonds.

Mandy felt full of hope as she biked down the street and turned into the quiet road that led to Lilac Cottage.

She left her bike by the gate. There was no sign of Grandma or Grandpa. Mandy hurried up the garden path. She went around the back; the greenhouse door was closed.

Mandy's heart thumped as she opened the door and went inside. She stood and stared at the bowl for a second or two. Then, hardly daring to breathe, she reached down and carefully lifted off the cover.

"Oh!" Mandy's heart thudded with excitement. The egg had cracked in half, and there, in the middle, was a tiny, beautiful, fluffy brownish-yellow duckling.

The duckling lay in the grass cuttings, tired from its hard job of pecking through the eggshell. It stirred and shook its little head. Then it opened its bright, beady eyes.

"Ohhh," Mandy breathed again. "Hello, little one." She stretched out her fingertip and gently touched its downy head. It cheeped

softly, dark eyes staring at her through the glass. "Welcome to Welford," Mandy whispered.

She heard a sound behind her and turned to see Grandpa standing in the doorway.

"Come and see, Grandpa!" Mandy said.

Grandpa crouched down beside her. "Well, hello, little thing."

Mandy's eyes were shining as she looked at him. "You *are* clever, Grandpa."

He grinned. "Blackie's the clever one, really."

"Yes." Mandy gazed at the duckling. "I'm going to call her Dillon," she said.

As she said the name, the duckling shook itself and got to its feet, cheeping loudly.

"It said in my book that ducklings don't need food for a while after they've hatched," Mandy said. "But she sounds pretty hungry to me."

"I wonder what ducklings eat," Grandpa said.

"Wild ducklings eat waterweed and things they find in the pond," Mandy told him. "I'll get James, and we'll go and get some."

"What about school?" Grandpa asked.

"Oh . . . well . . . after school."

By now, Grandma had arrived to see the new baby.

"Isn't she cute!" She bent down beside Mandy and Grandpa. "I thought she'd be yellow all over."

"So did I," Mandy said. "But I suppose her mom was brown, so she has some brown on her, too."

"Yes, I suppose," Grandpa said. He stood up. "But you can't always be going off to the pond to find food for her, Mandy." He turned to Grandma. "Why don't you call Kathy, Dorothy? She might be able to suggest something else we could feed her."

"It's a little early," Grandma replied, still gazing at Dillon. "She'll be out feeding her chickens. I'll call her later and let you know after school, Mandy. I'm sure Dillon will be all right until then."

Mandy could hardly bear to leave. "You *will* keep an eye on her for me, won't you?" she begged.

Grandma gave her a quick hug. "Of course we will, and I'll get whatever duckling food Kathy suggests."

As Mandy turned to walk away, Dillon gave a loud cheep and tried to climb out of the bowl.

"I'll find her a box now that she's hatched," Grandpa said. "She'll need something bigger than the bowl."

"Thanks, Grandpa. That'll be great." Mandy glanced at her watch. If she hurried she'd have time to run back home to tell Mom and Dad the good news. She couldn't go to James's house this early. He never got up until the last minute.

Her heart was beating fast as she sped off on her bike toward Animal Ark. What a fantastic day!

5

The New Arrival

Mandy was so excited that when she turned onto the street that would take her to Animal Ark she almost collided with Della Skilton.

"Hey, careful, Mandy!" Della laughed.

Della was the manager of Westmoor House, a retirement home for old people. She was carrying a young black cat in a basket.

"Oh, sorry!" Mandy panted. She eyed the basket anxiously. "Is Pepper sick?"

"She hasn't been felling well, so I'm taking her for a checkup. Nothing serious, I'm sure."

"That's good." Mandy didn't have the time to stop and tell her about Dillon. "I'd walk with you, but I'm in a rush," she explained.

"So I see." Della smiled and waved as Mandy raced on ahead.

At Animal Ark she pushed open the gate, scooted up the path, dumped her bike against the wall, and dashed into the clinic.

The receptionist, Jean Knox, was just taking the cover off her computer. She looked up in surprise as Mandy hurtled through the door. "Mandy! What on earth's the matter?"

"The baby's been born," Mandy panted. "Are Mom and Dad both still here?"

"Baby?" Jean looked more surprised than ever. "I didn't know anyone in Welford was having a baby."

Mandy laughed. "Oh, no . . . our duckling, she's been born — hatched, I mean."

Jean clapped her hands. "How wonderful."

Dr. Emily walked in from the back. "Mandy! I thought you already left."

"I did." Mandy's eyes were shining. "Now I'm back to tell you the baby's born."

"Baby? Oh . . . the duckling!" Dr. Emily exclaimed. "That's wonderful."

"She's beautiful. I'm calling her Dillon," Mandy said.

"Dillon?" Her dad came out from the storage closet carrying a box of medicine. "Do you think a girl will be pleased to have a name like Dillon?"

Mandy looked determined. "It can be a girl's name and a boy's name," she said. "There's a boy in our class named Dillon. Actually he's a bully, but I'm sure this Dillon won't be like that with other ducks."

"Okay," Dr. Adam said. "Dillon it is."

Everyone burst out laughing, and Mandy knew from the twinkle in her dad's eye that he was only teasing.

JEAN KNOX

Just then Della arrived with her kitten. Then someone else turned up with a rabbit in a cardboard box. Clinic hours had started, and it was time for Mandy to go to school.

"I'm going to see Dillon after school," she called as Dr. Emily and Dr. Adam went through to the back to begin the day's work. "So I'll be home late."

"All right," Dr. Emily called. "Now, don't be a nuisance if Grandma and Grandpa are busy."

Mandy was already halfway out the front door. "I won't."

She met James coming across the green. "It's here!" she shouted even before she reached him. "The baby's been born."

James's face was bursting with excitement. "When?" he said. "What's it like? How big is it? What color is it? Is it all right?"

Mandy answered all his questions on the way to school. "And I'm calling her Dillon," she said as they reached the school gates. "Good, don't you think?"

"Yes," said James. "I can't wait to see her."

* * *

All day, school seemed to drag. Mandy thought the day would never end.

The bell finally rang for dismissal, and Mandy was the first out. She waited impatiently for James by the school gate. When he arrived, they both pedaled like the wind to Lilac Cottage.

When they got there, there was an old blue van in the driveway. Grandma was coming out of the greenhouse with a tall, gray-haired woman.

Grandma introduced her. "This is my friend Kathy."

"Hello. I'm sorry about your cat," Mandy said, remembering Grandpa's conversation with Kathy on the phone.

Grandma's friend looked sad. "Thank you, my dear," she replied. "But Snowball had a good, long life. He was eighteen, you know."

"Wow!" James said. "Eighteen. *Twice* as old as you, Mandy. That's *really* old."

Grandma and Kathy couldn't help smiling.

"You must really miss him," Mandy said.

"Yes," Kathy replied sadly. "I do."

"Kathy's brought some food for Dillon," Grandma said.

"Chick crumbs," Kathy said.

"Chick crumbs?" James burst out.

"Yes, chick crumbs. They're fine for ducklings, too," Kathy said.

"Oh, thank you!" Mandy took the bag gratefully, and she and James went into the greenhouse to see Dillon.

"She's so cute!" James said as he crouched to stroke Dillon's downy head.

Dillon was cheeping loudly.

"She must be starving by now," Mandy said. "I'll ask Grandma if she's got an old saucer we can put her food on."

Grandma and Kathy had gone into the kitchen to make a cup of tea. Grandma gave Mandy an old saucer for the duckling.

"We'll come and see her have her first dinner," Grandma said.

They followed Mandy back to the green-house, and Mandy put a handful of chick crumbs onto the saucer. Then she lifted Dillon carefully out of her box. The little duckling began gobbling the food up right away.

Mandy laughed. "She *was* hungry, wasn't she?"

After she filled up with chick crumbs, Dillon settled herself down next to Mandy's feet.

James laughed. "She likes you, Mandy. She's snuggled up to your shoes."

Behind them, Kathy was smiling broadly. "I bet I know what's happened," she said.

"What?" Mandy and James asked together.

"Were you there when she hatched?" Kathy asked Mandy.

Mandy shook her head. "No, but I was the first one to see her."

"And she was in your grandma's glass bowl?"

"Yes," Mandy said, puzzled.

"Well," Kathy said. "I believe she's imprinted on your shoes."

"*Imprinted?*" James frowned.

Mandy explained quickly what it meant.

Grandpa had been listening. He chuckled. "So Dillon thinks Mandy is her mom."

But Grandma shook her head. "No, that's not right, Tom," she said with a broad grin. "Dillon thinks Mandy's *shoes* are her mom."

James snorted and burst out laughing.

"It's not funny," Mandy said seriously. "How would you like a pair of school shoes for a mother!"

6

An Argument

Mandy and James stayed with Dillon for a while. Grandpa had found a little water dish for Dillon, too. She had drunk some of the water, dipping in her tiny beak, then putting her head up to swallow it. Mandy thought Dillon was the most adorable animal she had ever seen.

Mandy then realized that she was hungry,

too. She decided it was time to go home for a snack. James agreed. She put Dillon back into her box and put the water beside her. "There you are, Dillon," she said. "Now, be good."

They quickly closed the greenhouse door behind them to keep in the warmth. Then they went to the kitchen to say good-bye to Grandma and Grandpa.

"And thanks for the duckling food," Mandy said to Kathy.

"You're welcome, my dear," Kathy replied. She was sitting at the kitchen table with Grandma counting the money they had collected to pay for the guided tour of Woodbridge Farm Park. "But you know she can't live in your grandpa's greenhouse forever," she added gently. "She'll need a pen and water to swim in. And grass and waterweed to peck at."

"That's true," James said.

Mandy sighed again. "I know."

"See what your mom and dad think," Grandma suggested.

Mandy's heart sank. "Yes," she said. "I will."

Although she had the feeling she knew exactly what they would say. Animal Ark was too busy to have Dillon around.

Grandma must have seen Mandy's sad face. "Don't worry," she said. "We'll figure out something. Dillon's all right here for a while." She got up and gave her granddaughter a quick hug.

Mandy and James walked together down to the village green.

"See you tomorrow," James said as they went their separate ways.

Mandy waved good-bye and set off for home. Her mind was in a whirl. What *was* she going to do with Dillon? Ducklings grew quickly . . . they needed to be with other ducks. Maybe she should wait a day or two and then take Dillon back to Millers Pond.

Mandy sighed again as she pushed open the gate to Animal Ark and went up the path. She would have to talk it over with Mom and Dad. Even if she couldn't keep Dillon at home, they would know what to do.

In the waiting room, Jean was putting the cover on her computer, getting ready to go home. Dr. Adam was in an examining room. To Mandy's surprise she could hear him arguing with someone. Dad hardly ever raised his voice or lost his temper. He did get annoyed with people who didn't take good care of their animals, but he usually managed to keep calm. This time, though, seemed to be different.

"It's no good, Mr. Taylor," he was saying. "I won't do it and that's that. You'll have to find another solution."

Just then, Dr. Emily came into the waiting room to check if there were any more patients to be seen.

"Mandy!" she said. "You're back. How's Dillon?"

"She's great. Mom, you must go and see her."

"I intend to," replied Dr. Emily. "This evening, in fact, if there aren't any emergency calls."

Loud voices were still coming from Dr.

Adam's room. Dr. Emily looked at Jean and shrugged her shoulders.

"What's going on?" Mandy asked.

Her mom shrugged again. "I'm not sure. A man came in with a cat, disappeared into the examining room, and I've heard arguing ever since."

"The man is Mr. Taylor. He lives in one of those new houses at Orchard Farm Close," Jean said. "It used to be a beautiful apple orchard when I was a girl."

"What's wrong with the cat?" Mandy asked.

Jean shook her head. "No idea. Mr. Taylor just demanded to see a vet, so I sent him into your father's examining room."

Just then the examining room door flew open. A short, dark, red-faced man wearing a business suit and shiny black shoes walked into the waiting room.

"Give me the number of the animal shelter," he demanded of Jean.

Mandy could see a small cat inside the carrying case, a Siamese kitten who was only about ten months old. She could just see its beautiful, vivid eyes. They looked scared as they peered through the wire mesh at the front of the carrying case.

"There's no point," Jean said calmly. "Miss Hilder is on vacation, and the person looking after things can't take any animals until she gets back."

"How long will that be?" the man snapped. He dumped the case at his feet and leaned his elbows on the counter. Before Jean could answer, his mobile phone rang. He took it out of his pocket.

"Yes . . . no . . . no. I'm at the vet's, and I've got to go back home before I come to work. I'll be about half an hour." He switched it off and put it back in his pocket.

"Well?" he said to Jean. "How long will the woman be away?"

"Two weeks," Dr. Emily told him.

"Two weeks?" The man suddenly seemed to notice her and Mandy standing there staring at him. He heaved a sharp sigh. "All right." He

picked up the basket, bumping it against the door as he barged through. "I'll find somewhere else," he said over his shoulder.

Dr. Adam was red in the face when he came into the waiting room. "That man!" he said angrily.

Mandy desperately wanted to know what they had been arguing about. But she wanted to tell her dad about Dillon, too. The news about the duckling came out first. Her words tumbled over one another until Dr. Adam held up his hand, a broad grin replacing the angry look on his face.

"Hold your horses, Mandy. Dillon thinks your shoes are *what*?"

"Her mother!" Mandy replied.

"Well, I think that's really sweet," Jean commented. She put her glasses in her bag and headed toward the door.

"So do I," Dr. Emily smiled. "You saved her life, so you deserve to be her mom."

"You mean her shoes do," Dr. Adam said,

grinning. He had calmed down now that the man with the cat had left.

"Yes," Mandy said. "But *I'll* be wearing the shoes, so it's up to me to keep her safe. Just as a real mother would do."

"Well," Dr. Emily said after dinner, when Mandy asked her about finding a proper home for Dillon, "you know we really haven't got time to look after Dillon here."

Mandy *did* know, of course, but she argued just the same. "One little duckling won't take much looking after," she said.

"No, that's true," Dr. Emily replied. "But someone needs to be here. Dad and I are busy; you're at school. What would Dillon do on her own all day?"

Mandy sighed. "Yes, you're right, Mom," she said unhappily. "We'll just have to take her back to Millers Pond, that's all . . . when she's big enough, of course."

Dr. Adam was reading the *Walton Gazette*. When he heard Mandy mention Millers Pond he looked up and shook his head. "That's no good, Mandy. She couldn't survive in the wild now, she's too used to human beings. She's lost her instinct for survival."

"Anyway," her mom added, "the other ducks might attack her. No, Mandy, we'll have to find another solution."

Dr. Adam had gone back to his paper. "Well, I never!" he suddenly exclaimed. "It's Mr. Taylor."

"Mr. Taylor?" Dr. Emily asked, frowning.

"The man with the cat," her husband reminded her.

Dr. Emily peered over her husband's shoulder. "What's he in the paper for?"

Dr. Adam read aloud. "'Paul Taylor, manager of the Walton Shoe Company, has been given the job of setting up a new business in the United States. He and his wife will move to Boston.'" He looked up. "He told me he was leaving Welford. That's why he wanted that young Siamese put to sleep."

Mandy's hand flew to her mouth in horror. "Put to sleep!"

"Shocking!' Dr. Emily said. "Why can't he simply find the poor creature another home?"

Dr. Adam shook his head. "He didn't think he'd be able to because —"

Just then the phone rang. Dr. Adam got up to answer it and came back looking grim. "That was Grandpa, Mandy. You'd better get up to Lilac Cottage right away. Dillon's got out of her box, and they can't find her anywhere."

7

Where's Dillon?

Mandy ran out of the house. She grabbed her bike and pedaled furiously to Lilac Cottage. Dillon missing? Where could she have gone?

Her heart beat faster. If Dillon met a cat . . . the woman next door to Grandma and Grandpa had a cat, a fierce ginger cat that was always catching baby birds. And sometimes a fox would venture onto the village green. She couldn't bear thinking about it.

In the cottage garden, Grandpa was on his hands and knees with his head in the shrubbery. All Mandy could see was his bottom and his legs sticking out.

"Dillon . . . good duck . . . come on, where are you?" he called.

Grandma was at the other end of the garden, trying to see behind the shed. A pile of old flowerpots and plastic seed trays was behind the shed, and Dillon might be hiding there. She was calling, too. "Dillon . . . nice duck . . . where are you?"

"When did you realize she was missing?" Mandy gasped.

Grandpa backed out of the shrubbery and looked up. "Only a few minutes ago. The greenhouse door was open just a tiny bit, enough for her to squeeze through." He sat back on his heels. "I'm sorry, Mandy. She's as lively as a monkey, that's for sure."

Mandy turned around and around. Dillon

could be anywhere in the garden. She could even have gone off down the street. Mandy had an awful feeling she knew why Dillon had escaped. She was looking for Mandy's shoes. Nature told Dillon to follow them wherever they went.

Through the greenhouse glass Mandy could see Dillon's box. It contained everything she needed . . . except a mother. Mandy bit her lip. She felt guilty. *She* had been the one to rescue Dillon; *she* should have been looking after her, not Grandma and Grandpa. "Oh, Dillon, where are you?" she murmured. "Please be safe."

"I'll look out in the street," Mandy called, making her way back down the path, looking in between the shrubs and flowers as she went. Then she went through the gate and up and down the road. Surely Dillon couldn't have gone far.

Up and down, up and down the road Mandy trudged. But there was no sign of Dillon anywhere. She went back to Lilac Cottage close to tears.

Grandpa had climbed the fence at the back of the garden and gone off toward the community gardens.

Grandma was sitting on the garden seat looking upset. "I'm so sorry, Mandy," she said. She shook her head. "I went in to look at Dillon, and I must have left the greenhouse door open a tiny bit. I'm so sorry."

Mandy sat beside her and gave her a hug. "You're a terrific grandma, and everyone makes mistakes. Dillon is my duckling. *I* should be the one taking care of her, not you."

Mandy made up her mind that if they did find Dillon safe and sound she would ask Mom and Dad again if she could keep her at Animal Ark. It would only be for a little while. Until they found her a new home.

She left Grandma and went back into the greenhouse. The box looked so empty without Dillon. There was a little hollow in the straw where the duckling had made herself comfortable.

Mandy had the horrible feeling she might never see Dillon again. She burst into tears.

She was just blowing her nose when she heard a sound — a strange sound. A rustle . . . a cheep.

She looked down just as a little beak popped out from behind one of Grandpa's tomato plants.

Cheep, cheep!

And Dillon came running out. She had seen Mandy's shoes. In fact, Mandy decided afterward, they were just what she had been waiting for.

"Grandma, Grandpa!" Mandy scooped the tiny animal up in her hands. "She's here! She's all right. Come and see!"

Grandpa came hurrying up the front path. He had gone all the way around the back, through the community gardens, and out into the road. Dr. Emily was with him. She was hurrying from Animal Ark to see what she could do to help.

"Thank goodness!" Grandma touched Dillon's tiny, downy head with her fingertip. She looked at Mandy's mom. Her eyes were shining with tears. "Oh, Emily, I would never have forgiven myself if anything had happened to her."

Dr. Emily was gazing at Dillon. It was the first time she had seen her, and Mandy could tell she was enchanted, too.

At last her mom gave a huge sigh. "Okay, Mandy," she said. "You win. You're right. *You* were the one to rescue Dillon, *you* should be the one looking after her."

Mandy gave a little cry. "Oh, thanks, Mom. She won't be a problem, honestly. And James will help me, I know he will. We'll feed her and clean out her box and take her for walks."

Dr. Emily smiled. "I don't think you need to take a duckling for walks, Mandy. Feeding and cleaning will probably be enough."

Grandpa found a makeshift lid for the box so they could carry Dillon home.

Mandy chatted excitedly as they made their way back to Animal Ark. "She could go in the shed, couldn't she? She'd be quite safe in there. I'll go to the church rummage sale on Saturday and find her an old plastic bowl to swim in."

Dr. Emily smiled again. "Great idea, Mandy. Remember, she can't stay in the shed forever. She needs fresh air and sunshine. We'll ask your dad to make a little run for her out on the lawn."

At home, Dr. Adam said that would be no trouble at all. "In fact," he said to Mandy when Dillon had been put safely in the shed for the night, "I've got some chicken wire somewhere. I'll find it tomorrow if I have time."

Mandy hugged him as tight as she could. "Oh, thanks, Dad. You're the best dad in the world." She hugged her mom, too. "And you're the best mom."

"What, better than a pair of school shoes?" Dr. Emily asked with a twinkle in her eye.

Before she went to bed Mandy wrote in *Duckling Diary*. There were so many exciting things to tell that she filled up two whole pages.

Next morning, Mandy fed Dillon, cleaned out her box, and gave her fresh water and a saucer of chick crumbs. Dillon settled down to eat them, but when Mandy tried to leave she ran cheeping behind her.

"Now, stay there," Mandy commanded. She picked her up gently and put her back by her saucer.

But when she turned to go, Dillon was right behind her. Mandy was so charmed she couldn't help letting Dillon follow her into the house so her mom and dad could see. She walked through the garden, up the step, and into the kitchen with Dillon right behind her.

Dr. Emily was getting ready for clinic hours.

Mandy danced around the kitchen with Dillon cheeping behind her and flapping her little wings.

Dr. Emily laughed helplessly, and Mandy's dad came out of his study to see what all the noise was about.

"I don't know!" He shook his head and grinned broadly. "This place is more like a zoo than a veterinary practice."

Still laughing, Mandy picked Dillon up gently and took her back out to the shed. "Sorry, Dillon," she said and put her into her box. "Dad will make that pen for you as soon as he can."

She had read in her library book that in the wild, ducklings swim around with their mom within a few days of hatching. The sooner she got that bowl so that Dillon had somewhere to swim, the better.

Just then, James came over. Mandy had called him the evening before to tell him Dillon was at Animal Ark. He'd insisted on saying hello to Dillon before they went to school.

James was bending down to pat Dillon when Dr. Emily called from the kitchen. "I'm off on my calls now, Mandy. Hurry up, or you'll both be late for school."

They said good-bye to Dillon and shut the shed door firmly. Back indoors Mandy packed her schoolbag, grabbed her lunch box, and then she and James walked across the green.

Outside the general store Mrs. McFarlane was sweeping the pavement in front of the door. She laughed when she saw Mandy and James. Mandy waved. "Morning, Mrs. McFarlane."

"Are you taking your friend to school?" Mrs. McFarlane called.

James screwed up his nose. "Does she mean me? I'm old enough to go to school by myself, thank you!"

Mandy laughed. "I don't know what she means."

Then Jean Knox pulled up outside the general store and got out of her car.

"Hi, Jean!" Mandy called. "We've got Dillon at home now!"

Jean just stood and stared. "Oh, no, you haven't," she called. "You've got her right be-hind you."

And when Mandy and James turned around, there was Dillon waddling frantically across the green. She was trying desperately to keep up with their strides.

"Oh, no! How did she get out?" Mandy ran and picked her up, cradling the duckling in her hands.

James shook his head. "We made sure the door was shut. There must be a hole in the shed somewhere."

"Oh, dear," Mandy said. "I should have checked. What *are* we going to do with you?" she murmured to the duckling. "I'd better take her back," she said to James.

But just then Mrs. Todd pulled up in her car. She looked puzzled to see Mandy heading for home instead of school.

Mandy explained. "Dillon followed me," she told her teacher. "You see, she thinks my shoes are her mother."

"Oh . . . I see," Mrs. Todd said, although she didn't look as if she understood at all. "Well, since she is here, why don't you bring her to school, so everyone can meet her?"

Mandy's eyes shone. "Oh, may I?" Everyone in her class knew about Dillon, and she had been dying to show her off.

"Just for the morning," Mrs. Todd said. "I'm sure we will be able to find a box for her. You can take her home at lunchtime. We've all heard so much about Dillon, everyone will be pleased to see her."

"Hear that, Dillon?" Mandy said, holding the soft animal against her cheek. "You're the most famous duckling in Welford!"

8

James's Brilliant Idea

Mrs. Todd was right. Everyone *was* pleased to see Dillon.

And Mandy was right, too. Dillon was indeed the most famous duckling in Welford. In fact, she was a star. And when Mandy showed everyone how she followed her shoes wherever she went, they thought it was the funniest thing they had ever seen.

Mrs. Todd had called Animal Ark to explain that Dillon had escaped and Mandy would be bringing her back at lunchtime. James got permission to go home with Mandy.

When James and Mandy arrived at Animal Ark, the shed door was still firmly shut. And sure enough, when they checked, there was a hole in the corner where the wood had rotted away.

"We'd better block it up," James said.

They found an old wooden box on a shelf in the back and wedged it firmly against the hole. While Mandy was feeding Dillon, James checked to see if there were any more holes.

Satisfied at last that Dillon was safe, they settled her in her box and closed the door behind them.

Dillon cheeped madly. Mandy hated leaving her. "She seems so unhappy," she wailed to James. "I wish I could stay with her all day."

Then James came up with the answer. "Wear your sneakers," he said, "and leave your school shoes here with Dillon. Then she'll be happy."

Mandy's face lit up. "James, what a *brilliant* idea!"

She ran upstairs to change into her sneakers. She knew she wasn't really supposed to wear them to school but hoped Mrs. Todd wouldn't mind. After all, Dillon's happiness was at stake.

Dr. Emily and Dr. Adam had come in from work to grab a sandwich for lunch.

Her mom spotted the sneakers at once. "Mandy, where are your school shoes?" she asked with a frown.

Mandy explained.

"Well," her mom said with a sigh. "I suppose it won't hurt to wear your sneakers for a day or two. And you need new school shoes anyway. We'll try to get to Walton this weekend to buy you some new ones."

"So it's all right to leave my shoes with Dillon? Oh, thanks, Mom!" Mandy hugged her. "I knew you'd understand."

Mandy and James ran out to the shed.

"Here you are, Dillon." Mandy put her shoes into the box. Dillon gave a cheep, fluffed out her feathers, and settled down, looking happy as could be.

"There," James said. "What did I tell you?"

"You *are* brilliant, James," Mandy said.

When Mandy arrived home from school that afternoon there was a message from Grandpa. They had found an old plastic baby bath that Dillon could have as a swimming pool. Grandpa used it to wash his flowerpots in, but he cleaned it up for Dillon. Mandy wouldn't have to wait for the rummage sale after all.

There was another surprise, too. Dr. Adam had found time to make Dillon's run. He also made a little house from another wooden box he found at the back of the shed.

"That's great, Dad." Mandy beamed when she saw it. "Dillon's going to love it."

Dr. Adam grinned, although he shook his head at the same time. "We don't want her to love it *too* much, Mandy. We have to find her somewhere to go where she can be with other ducks."

Mandy's face fell. "I know, Dad. I've been thinking about it for ages."

Dr. Adam put his arm across her shoulders. "Well, try not to worry, honey. We'll find a place."

Mandy thought hard as she carried Dillon to her new pen. The trouble was, she couldn't think of *anywhere*.

Dillon seemed delighted with her new house and run. She waddled around, cheeping and pecking at the grass. Then she ran into her little house and ran out again.

Mandy gazed at her dad. "She loves it, Dad. Thanks."

Mandy placed her shoes next to Dillon's house and stood up with a sigh. There was just enough time to write in her diary and go to Lilac Cottage before dinner.

She went upstairs to her room, took her diary from her desk, and began to write. The pages were almost filled. She wrote about how Dillon had followed her to school and how much everyone had loved her. She drew a little picture of Dillon in her pen, sitting with Mandy's shoes.

When she turned the page she realized that there were only two pages left. Soon it would be time to take the diary to school to show Mrs. Todd. It made her feel sad. The last entry would have to be about Dillon's new home. She bit her lip. If *only* she could think of somewhere Dillon would be safe and happy.

Mandy sighed, put her diary away, and went downstairs. She popped her head in the clinic door to tell her mom she was off to Lilac Cottage.

"Cheer up, Mandy," Dr. Emily said. "Dillon's all right, isn't she?"

Mandy sighed again. "Yes, she's fine."

"Good," her mom said.

On her way to her grandparents', several people stopped to ask how Dillon was. It seemed her fame had spread even wider.

"She's fine," Mandy told Mr. Hadcroft, the vicar. "But I've got to find her a new home soon. She needs to be with other ducks."

Mr. Hadcroft looked thoughtful. "If I hear of anyone who can provide a suitable home for her, I'll let you know," he said.

Another man came walking down the road. Mandy recognized him at once. It was Mr. Taylor, the man who wanted his cat put to sleep. He was hurrying toward the post office with a bundle of letters in his hand.

"Hello, Mr. Taylor," Mandy said. She just *had* to find out about his cat.

Mr. Taylor stopped, frowning. He was red in the face and obviously in a hurry. "Do I know you, young lady?"

Mandy told him who she was.

When he heard she was the daughter of the vets he looked a bit sheepish. "Oh," he said. "Well, I still haven't decided what to do with LaLa."

"LaLa?" It was the strangest name for a cat Mandy had ever heard.

"We called her that because when she me-ows she sounds as if she's singing," he explained. He sighed. "I know my wife's going to be really upset but it seems the kindest thing."

"Why?" Mandy said indignantly. "LaLa's not sick, is she?"

Mr. Taylor frowned. "Didn't your father tell you?"

Mandy shook her head. "No."

"She's deaf, poor thing. I really didn't think anyone would want her, and we just can't take her to America with us." He waved his hand and hurried away. "Sorry, young lady, I must go mail these letters."

Mandy stared after him. Deaf? Well, that wasn't the end of the world. Mr. Taylor just hadn't tried hard enough, that was all. Poor LaLa!

She ran to Lilac Cottage. She couldn't wait to get the baby bath for Dillon to swim in.

Grandpa was in his workshop fixing a broken chair. Grandma was on her outing to Wood-bridge Farm Park.

"It's in the kitchen," Grandpa told Mandy when she asked about the baby bath. "Good as new and waiting for you."

"Thanks, Grandpa," Mandy said. She ran indoors to get it.

She took the bath home and filled it with water. Dillon cheeped so loudly when Mandy lifted her up to see it that Mandy thought the duckling might explode.

The sides were too high for Dillon to climb in and out, so Mandy found a piece of wood to make a ramp. Soon Dillon was swimming happily around. She ducked and dived, splashing her feathers. Then she began preening herself. Mandy knew from her book that this would begin to make her feathers waterproof. "Oiling up" it was called. Ducks had to do it, otherwise their feathers would soak up the water, and the ducks would sink.

After dinner Mandy had time to write in her diary about Dillon and her new bath before James arrived with Blackie. They played with Dillon for a while, and then Mandy found a

couple of empty jam jars to fill with water-weed. They put on their boots and set off for Millers Pond.

"Be careful," Dr. Emily called as they went out.

"We will," they replied.

"Dillon's got to learn how to peck at water-weed," Mandy said as they walked. "She needs to be ready for when we find her a *real* pond to be her home."

They made their way up the street and around the edge of the field that led to the pond. A bird was sitting in the willow tree, and dragonflies whirred over the surface like bright little helicopters. A couple of moorhens were exploring the long grass. They ran away and splashed into the water when Mandy and James arrived.

After they tied Blackie to a tree in case he decided to start chasing things, Mandy and James went to the shallow end of the pond. They scooped up handfuls of waterweed. One or two pond snails were stuck to the trailing roots. Mandy carefully picked them off and put them back into the water.

They had filled both jam jars when James suddenly whispered, "Hey . . . look!"

Mandy looked up and saw a dark brown duck emerging from the overhanging willow. Behind her swam four ducklings. Three were dark, and one was a pale, downy yellow.

Mandy drew in her breath. "Oh, aren't they gorgeous?"

"There must have been another nest," James said. "If it was a fox that destroyed Dillon's nest, at least it didn't find this one."

"Thank goodness," Mandy breathed.

They watched the little family for a while and then crept quietly away.

"That's what Dillon should have been doing," Mandy said sadly as they made their way home. "Swimming around with her mom and brothers and sisters."

"I know." James felt sad, too.

"Not splashing around in an old baby bath," Mandy added.

James sighed. "Too bad we can't bring her back here."

"I know," Mandy said. "But I'm sure Dad's right. She's too used to humans to survive in the wild now. We've just got to find her somewhere with other ducks but where there are humans, too. The trouble is, I just can't think of anywhere."

"No," James said, looking glum. "Neither can I."

9

A Problem Solved?

Back home, Mandy put one jam jar full of waterweed into Dillon's bath, keeping the other
jar of weed for the next day.

When Dillon went up her little ramp and
jumped into the water, Mandy pecked at the
weed with her finger to show the duckling

what to do. Dillon soon got the idea. She gobbled it up and loved it.

"It'll do her good to get wild food," Mandy said. "She can't live on chick crumbs for ever."

After Dillon ate all the weed, they put her away safely in her little house for the night.

"I'll walk home with you if you like," Mandy said to James. "Then we can drop by to thank Grandma for the bath on the way."

Mandy and James made their way toward Lilac Cottage. Mrs. Ponsonby was sitting on the seat on the village green enjoying the evening sunshine. Pandora, her overweight Pekingese dog, was sitting beside her.

Mrs. Ponsonby got up when she saw Mandy and James and came toward them. The feather in her hat waved in the breeze. Pandora waddled beside her, her tail waving like a flag. "How's that little pet of yours? Lillian, is it?" She was a little out of breath when she spoke.

"Dillon," Mandy smiled. "She's fine, thank you."

Mrs. Ponsonby sniffed. "I like ducks. I wanted to go on that Women's Club outing today, but they wouldn't allow me to take Pandora to the farm, would they, darling?" she said to the dog who sat panting at her feet. "How silly," Mrs. Ponsonby went on. "She wouldn't have chased anything, would you, sweetheart?"

Pandora made a strange noise, a cross between a snuffle and a sneeze. It sounded exactly like the word *no*.

When they were out of earshot, Mandy couldn't help giggling. "I can't imagine Pandora chasing anything, can you? She's far too fat."

James shook his head. "Only a chocolate cookie, and only if you threw it to her."

Mandy laughed again, and they continued on to Lilac Cottage.

Kathy's van was parked outside. She and Grandma had just come back from their trip to the farm park. They were sitting at the kitchen table drinking mugs of tea and looking at some pamphlets.

"Did you have a nice time at the farm?" Mandy and James asked after they thanked Grandma for the baby bath.

"Oh, it was wonderful," Grandma said. "Wasn't it, Kathy?"

"It really was," Kathy agreed. "They've got a wonderful herd of Jersey cows."

"I love Jersey cows," James said.

"We saw them being milked," Kathy told them. "It's all done by computer nowadays, you know. All the dairy farmer does is press buttons."

"Wow!" James said.

"They keep sheep, too," Grandma said. "And goats; even a llama."

"A llama!" Mandy exclaimed.

"He was very friendly," Grandma said. "People breed them for their wool, you know, although this one is more like a pet."

"What else do they have?" Mandy asked.

Grandma stood up to get the lemonade and cookies. "A small animal corner with rabbits and gerbils and guinea pigs," she told them.

Mandy sighed. "I'd love to see them."

"Grandpa promised to take you, didn't he?" Grandma said. She put two glasses of lemonade and the cookie tin in front of them.

"Yes," Mandy said.

"Well, then, he will," Grandma reassured her.

Kathy was still reading one of the brochures. On the front was a picture. It showed a wooden sign spelling out *Woodbridge Farm Park*. Behind the sign was a lake with a willow tree.

Mandy stared. Then she pointed to the picture. "Did you see any wild ducks on this lake?" she asked, excited.

"Yes. They come to feed with the farm ducks, but they're used to human beings and are very tame," Kathy replied.

Grandma suddenly seemed to realize what Mandy was getting at. And so did Kathy. A broad smile spread across her face. "Oh, Mandy, that would be the perfect place for Dillon!"

Mandy took a deep breath. "Do you think they would take her?"

Grandma picked up another brochure and found a phone number. "There's never any harm in asking," she said. "You don't get anywhere unless you ask." She handed the brochure to Mandy. "There's the number. Why don't you call them?"

Mandy went out into the hall and dialed the number. But there was no answer.

Grandma patted her shoulder. "I expect they're busy outside with the animals. Try again later."

Mandy sat down at the table and put her chin on her hands. "If they do take Dillon," she said, "I'll miss her so much."

"Yes, sweetheart," Grandma said. "But you know you can't keep her much longer."

"I know." Mandy sighed again.

"That's the trouble with having pets," Kathy said. "You miss them so much when they've gone." She had a little catch in her voice.

Mandy knew she was talking about her cat, Snowball.

"You could get another cat," James said. "But I don't think we'll get another duck, will we, Mandy?"

Mandy shook her head. "No."

"It's really difficult," Kathy said. "Especially with all my chicks. Snowball was a special cat, because he was deaf, you see."

"Ye-e-es." Mandy said slowly. An idea was coming into her head. A wonderful idea! Mr. Taylor's cat was special, too. So special that Mr. Taylor didn't think anyone would want her. But Mandy knew someone who would want her *because* she was deaf, like Snowball had been. LaLa wouldn't hear chicks cheeping and try to chase them. She was the perfect new pet for Kathy.

She jumped out of her chair suddenly. "Grandma, may I use the phone again?"

Grandma looked a bit startled. "Yes, of course, darling. But the people at the farm will probably still be busy."

"No, I need to ask Dad something," Mandy said.

"Well," Kathy said, and she got up, too. "I've got to go feed my hens."

"No, please wait a minute," Mandy said. "*Please* wait."

She ran out into the hall and dialed Animal Ark's number. If her dad had Mr. Taylor's address, she knew he would give it to her. And she *knew* Mr. Taylor would gladly give LaLa to Kathy.

But as she waited impatiently for someone to answer, her heart suddenly sank. Mr. Taylor had been desperate to get rid of the cat. What if it was already too late?

10

Another Problem Solved?

The phone at Animal Ark rang and rang. Mandy was just about to give up when she heard her mom's voice.

She explained breathlessly what she wanted.

"Hang on," her mom said. "I'll go and ask Dad."

She soon came back with Mr. Taylor's address and phone number.

Mandy scribbled it down quickly on the notepad by the phone. "Thanks, Mom."

"But why do you want it?" her mom asked.

"I'll tell you later. Bye!" Mandy put down the phone and ran back into the kitchen. But to her disappointment Kathy had gone.

"She couldn't wait," Grandma explained. "She said the hens would be starving."

"Let's see if we can catch her, James," Mandy said.

They rushed outside.

Luckily, Kathy was still at the gate. Grandpa had come back from visiting his friend, and she was telling him about their trip.

Kathy listened carefully as Mandy told her about Mr. Taylor and LaLa. When Mandy came to the part about him wanting the Siamese put to sleep, Kathy's hand flew to her mouth. "How horrible! Where did you say he lived?"

"Here." Mandy thrust the piece of paper in front of her.

"It's on my way home," Kathy said. "I think I'll pay him a visit. Would you like to come, you two? And Blackie, of course."

"Yes, please!" they said together.

"I'll call your mom to tell her where you've gone," Grandpa said.

"Could you call mine, too, please?" James said.

Grandpa promised he would, and they climbed into the van and set off.

The Taylors' house was one of four big new houses at the end of the village. The house had a long path leading to an oak door.

"Oh, no," Kathy said as they drew up outside. "It looks as if they've gone."

They stared at the house. There were no curtains at the windows, no car in the garage. It looked empty and deserted.

"They must be here," Mandy wailed. "I just saw Mr. Taylor yesterday."

But then a thin lady wearing jeans and a T-shirt came from around the back of the house with two black bags full of garbage. She came up the path and dumped them outside the front gate.

They all got out of the car.

"Mrs. Taylor?" Kathy asked.

The woman nodded.

Kathy told her who they were.

"And we wanted to know if you've still got LaLa," Mandy blurted out before she could stop herself."

"Yes," Kathy added. "Because I'd like to give her a home."

"Oh, would you?" Mrs. Taylor looked as if she was going to burst into tears. "I was so angry with my husband for taking her to see Dr. Adam. He said he just didn't know what else to do. You do know that she's . . . "

"Yes," Kathy said quickly. She told Mrs. Taylor about Snowball and the chicks. "So she'll be a perfect match," she said.

Five minutes later LaLa was in her carrying case on the backseat of Kathy's van.

LaLa stared at them with her huge, sky-blue eyes. Mandy poked her finger through the wire mesh and touched her silky head. "Don't worry, LaLa," she said. "You'll be all right now."

"She's very nervous," Mrs. Taylor said as she thanked them again.

"Don't worry," Kathy assured her. "With gentle handling and a lot of tender loving care, I'm sure she'll soon settle down."

She thanked Mrs. Taylor again and started the van. "I'll take you both to Animal Ark. I can make an appointment for LaLa to have a checkup at the same time."

At Animal Ark, Dr. Adam and Dr. Emily were delighted to hear the good news.

"Bring her in tomorrow morning," Dr. Adam said to Kathy when she dropped off Mandy and James at the front door. "I'll examine her then."

Mandy waved and Kathy hurried off to feed her hens. Then Mandy turned to her dad and told him about their plan for Dillon.

He smiled. "That's a great idea, Mandy."

"If they'll take her," she said.

"Let's try calling again," said James. "Then we'll know one way or the other."

"All right," Mandy agreed.

This time someone did answer. It was the farm manager. Mandy suddenly felt tongue-tied. It was a long story. And would he understand about her shoes?

"Dad," she said after telling the farm manager who she was. "Could you explain, please?"

Five minutes later Dr. Adam put the phone down. He had a broad grin on his face. "They'll be glad to have her," he said. "Tomorrow's Saturday, and we'll take her after morning clinic hours. Okay?"

Mandy threw her arms around him. "Oh, Dad, that's *great*!"

"However," Dr. Adam warned, "he said the

other ducks might give her a hard time at first."

"Dillon is very brave," James said. "She'll stick up for herself."

"Well, I hope so," Dr. Adam said. "And she'll miss your shoes, Mandy."

"I could leave them there," Mandy said.

Dr. Adam looked doubtful. "I don't know how. If you leave them on the bank, she might not want to swim. If you put them in the water, they'll sink."

"Oh, no." Mandy felt sad. Dad was right. She wanted Dillon to have a real home, other ducks to play with, and the right food to eat. But she didn't want her to be miserable.

Then she suddenly had an idea. Maybe Grandpa could help.

"I'd better get home," James was saying. "May I come with you tomorrow?"

"Of course you may," Mandy said. "Dillon would hate it if you weren't there to say good-bye."

After James left, Mandy called her grandpa. Grandpa listened carefully to what she had to say. Then he said, "Okay, Mandy. I'll see what I can do."

Mandy felt close to tears making the next-to-last entry in her *Duckling Diary*. She knew she would hate saying good-bye. But there were some things you just had to do. Some bridges you had to cross.

Before bed, she went to look in on Dillon. The little duckling was fast asleep, tucked up in her little house with one of Mandy's shoes. She opened one eye and gave a cheep when Mandy carefully lifted the lid to look at her.

Mandy touched the downy head with her finger. Dillon was growing fast. She would soon lose her baby feathers. She would soon stop cheeping and begin quacking. In fact, she would soon be a grown-up duck.

Mandy wiped away a tear, closed the lid softly, and went back inside the house.

Next morning, Grandpa and James arrived just as the last patient left the clinic. Mandy rushed out to greet them. "Grandpa, you've done it!" she cried when she saw the object Grandpa carried under his arm.

"Yes." Grandpa showed her. It was a little raft made from two short pieces of wood nailed together. Underneath, Grandpa had fixed two pieces of foam that would help the wood to stay afloat.

James frowned. "What is it?"

"It's a raft," Mandy explained. "Grandpa made it. We're going to float my shoes on it so Dillon will have them with her for as long as she wants."

Mandy's mom and dad looked amazed when they saw the raft.

"Whose idea was *that*?" Dr. Adam asked.

"Mine, of course," Mandy replied.

"I'm not sure it'll work," Dr. Emily began.

Mandy looked determined. "It will," she said. "I know it will."

Grandpa took some string from his pocket, and Mandy tied the shoes firmly to the raft.

"There," she said. "That should do the trick." Now all they had to do was go and get Dillon.

Mandy felt sad lifting the little duckling gently from her baby bath. She put her into the box she had lived in at Lilac Cottage and carried her out to where the others were waiting.

They all walked along the main street. Grandpa carried the raft, and Mandy had Dillon's box safely tucked under her arm.

The farm was on the road to Walton, just outside the village. When they arrived, Mr. Marsh, the farm manager, came out to greet them.

He shook hands with everyone and took a look at Dillon. "She's great," he said. "She looks very healthy." He turned to Mandy. "You've done a good job there, Mandy."

"And James," Mandy said quickly. "She's his duckling, too."

"You both did a great job," Mr. Marsh said. "Let's go down to the pond." Then he noticed the raft with the shoes attached to it. "What's that?"

He laughed when Mandy explained.

"It'll be all right, won't it?" she asked anxiously. "It won't scare the other ducks, will it?"

"I don't think so," Mr. Marsh assured her. "Come on, let's find out."

The lake was in the field behind the hay barn. It was shaped like a fat figure eight and had a weeping willow at one end. The edges were lined with long grass and huge yellow irises. Ducks and geese of all varieties were swimming around.

"We're really pleased the wild ducks come here to feed," Mr. Marsh said. "They mix with our own very well."

Dotted here and there were little duck houses with ramps going down into the water.

"They're safe from predators," Mr. Marsh explained. "Foxes will swim a little way to raid nests but not that far."

"We know," Mandy said sadly. "We think that's what happened to Dillon's brothers and sisters."

Mr. Marsh patted her shoulder. "Don't worry," he said. "She'll be safe here."

Several families of ducks were swimming in and out of the long grass. One came toward them as they stood by the edge.

"The ducklings in that little family are about the same age as Dillon," Mr. Marsh said, pointing to them. "Maybe she'll tag along with them."

Everyone held their breath when Mandy bent down and put the raft into the water.

"I'm not at all sure this is going to work," Grandpa said, biting his lip. Then he broke into a broad grin as the raft, plus shoes, floated perfectly. "There you are," he said. "I knew it would."

"Oh, Dad!" Dr. Emily said, laughing.

Grandpa winked at her and laughed, too.

Mandy opened the box and took Dillon out. The duckling sat in her hands, cheeping. Then she seemed to smell the water and the fresh air, because she raised her beak to the breeze and cheeped the loudest she ever had.

"You'd better put her in," Dr. Emily said gently. "The sooner the others see her, the better."

Mandy crouched down and spread her hands out over the surface of the water. Dillon took one look and jumped in with a little splash. She saw the raft and swam swiftly toward it, her little head bobbing back and forth.

The family of ducklings began swimming toward her.

As they closed in on Dillon, Mandy held her breath. Her heart seemed to be beating right up in her throat. "Please be all right," she whispered. "Please be all right."

She felt her mother's arm around her shoulders.

One of the ducklings, the biggest, suddenly flew at Dillon, cheeping. There was a swift flurry, a blur of ducklings, and splashing water. Then the others came closer to get a better view of what was going on.

"Oh, no," Mandy gasped. "They're going to hurt her."

But Dillon was much too brave for that. She swam away. Then she turned quickly and pecked the bigger duckling smartly on the tail. She turned and swam back rapidly toward the little raft. The other duckling followed her. The others arrived, and suddenly there was another flurry. It seemed the water was boiling with squabbling ducklings.

Then Dillon emerged. She swam around in circles, the others behind her. They soon lost interest and swam to the mother duck, who was waiting for them. Dillon climbed onto the raft, shook herself, and stood on it beside Mandy's shoes, watching the others.

On the bank, Mandy clasped her mother's hand tightly. Dillon *had* to go and swim with the others. It was great to have the shoes there, but she couldn't stay with them forever.

Then, suddenly, Dillon cheeped loudly and plunged into the water. She swam as fast as she could toward the other ducklings. They turned and stared at her. When they swam away toward the other side of the pond, Dillon followed them. Soon all five ducklings were playing together, splashing and diving, already the best of friends.

"Bye, Dillon," Mandy whispered, as everyone clapped and cheered. "Have a good time."

Her eyes were shining as she turned to James. "Wasn't she brave?"

"Yes," James agreed. "Brave and very smart."

They watched as Dillon and her new family disappeared into the reeds.

"She'll be fine," Mr. Marsh said with a sigh of relief. "She'll be absolutely fine."

"I think she's forgotten my shoes already," Mandy said. She turned to her Grandpa. "I'm sorry, Grandpa. Maybe you didn't need to make the raft after all."

Grandpa gave her a hug. "It's all right, Mandy. As long as Dillon is all right, nothing else matters."

And as they made their way back to the village, Mandy knew that what Grandpa said was true. "Well," she said with a sigh. "At least my *Duckling Diary* will have a happy ending."

When they got back home, James went off to get Blackie, and Mandy went to her room to write the very last page of her diary. She sighed as she wrote down the morning's events. She carefully drew a picture of the raft with her shoes attached to it and Dillon swimming away to join her new friends.

I was so proud of Dillon as she went off to play with her new duckling friends, she wrote. *I know she will be safe and happy. This is the end of my* Duckling Diary.

Mandy quickly read what she had written and closed the book with a sigh. She ran downstairs and out into the sunshine. It had been great looking after Dillon, but knowing the little duckling was in the best place she could possibly be was the nicest feeling of all.